THREE STREETS

STORYBOOK ND

CURATED BY GINI ALHADEFF

FORTHCOMING

THREE STREETS

YOKO TAWADA

translated from the Japanese
by Margaret Mitsutani

STORYBOOK ND

PUBLISHER'S NOTE: These three stories, "Kollwitzstrasse," "Majakowskiring,"
and "Puschkinallee," were selected from a volume originally published in Japanese
as *Hyakunen-no-sanpo* ("A Century of Walks,") by Shincho-sha in 2017. Published
by arrangement with the author

Manufactured in the United States of America
First published clothbound by New Directions in 2022

Library of Congress Cataloging-in-Publication Data
Names: Tawada, Yōko, 1960– author. | Mitsutani, Margaret, translator.
Title: Three streets / by Yoko Tawada ; translated from the Japanese
by Margaret Mitsutani.
Description: First edition. | New York : A Storybook ND, 2020.
Identifiers: LCCN 2020012674 | ISBN 9780811229302 (hardcover) |
ISBN 9780811229319 (ebook)
Subjects: LCSH: Tawada, Yōko, 1960– —Translations into English.
Classification: LCC PL862.A85 A2 2020 | DDC 895.63/5--dc23
LC record available at https://lccn.loc.gov/2020012674

10 9 8 7 6 5 4 3 2 1

New Directions Books are published for James Laughlin
by New Directions Publishing Corporation
80 Eighth Avenue, NY 10011

THREE STREETS

KOLLWITZSTRASSE

A child, still too little for school, is walking in an odd way, as if it's making its way across the surface of the moon. That puffy down jacket full of feathers is a space suit; in place of a helmet, a white knitted cap is pulled all the way down over its ears. One foot goes up and the whole body seems about to slide off diagonally into the air. But when the heel hits the ground, the child's whole weight comes down with a thud, threatening to throw it off balance—it stumbles, grabs the hem of its mother's coat, and gawks around, wide-eyed. The mother looks calmly down on her child. I stop to watch them, pretending to search for something in my pocket.

Invisible sensors extend from the child's forehead. The sensors move constantly, darting this way and that, trying to absorb all the stimuli from the outside world. Like those bicycles parked by the side of the road: they're an important source of information. Some have handlebars shaped like sheep horns, others like a bull's horns. Wondering if bicycles have zodiac signs, I look again and see one that resembles a goat, another a lion, and still another a scorpion.

The tiny lights on the child's shoes start to blink. This is not a human child, but a robot. The moment this thought occurs to me I take a leap into the future. I'd just read a dystopian novel in which children were no longer being born and the human race was heading for extinction. People were starting to demand child robots. Although software enabling robots to converse with human beings had been perfected long ago, the development of "my-child-robots"—with the capacity to use outside data organically, mixing it with their programs to form their own personalities—was stuck at a rudimentary level without much hope for improvement. Company A's robot, for instance, was very popular at first because it responded so sweetly to whatever its parents said, but in time the adults got sick of all that sweetness and stopped talking to it, leaving the child robot to gather dust in its own room, where it eventually stopped moving. Company B, on the other hand, came up with an intellectually curious type that peppered its parents with questions, storing up more and more knowledge. It was programmed with just the right amount of cheekiness and persistence, too. Unfortunately, it only asked things like "How many people live in this city?" and "What year was the French Revolution?" so the parents soon got bored and switched it off in irritation. There'd been something fascinating about the stuff real children had asked about long ago, but Company B failed to discover the source for questions like "Where is my dead uncle living now?" or "Why doesn't our dog talk?"

One research group concluded that inputting knowledge through parent-child conversations alone would be too difficult, so they developed software that absorbed a little information each day through sensors. Parents were instructed to take their "my-child-robot" with them wherever they went. If they took it shopping, for example, it would learn not only about the products sold in human society but also the difference between days when its parents dragged their feet, gloomy and distracted, and days when they smiled as they briskly marched along. But a good mood didn't guarantee that the parents would buy their child-robot whatever it wanted; sometimes, when they were too depressed to talk, they would buy it toys or chocolate cake. Little by little, the robot would have to learn how the weather affected people's moods. For instance, at twilight on a winter's day, when the sun, stubbornly hovering just above the horizon, suddenly drew a deep velvet curtain across itself, darkening the city, the parents' moods darkened too, until they went outside and saw fresh, clean snow sparkling in the glimmer of streetlamps, shining on the reds and oranges of winter scarves, and they would be enveloped in a brightness and warmth that comes only in winter. This, too, was important information about human society that would be carved into the child-robot's brain—information that couldn't be translated into digits, which is why Company C decided to use visual images. People's feelings, smells, the moisture in the air, the cold, and the light from streetlamps could all be captured in a single picture. But then they found that just putting a picture into a robot's brain was useless. First they'd need to program the brain with the capacity to appreciate the picture. So about halfway through, this dystopian novel ran smack into the mystery of what it means to be human.

The mother and child in front of me started walking

again, so I followed at the same pace. I saw a logo tag, small yet visible from a distance, sewn into the hood of the child's white down jacket, for a company that once specialized in mountaineering gear for alpine climbers but was now known for its top-of-the-line children's clothing. The jacket must have cost several hundred euros. In this area, there were people who thought nothing of shelling out a couple of thousand euros, or even five thousand, to get their child ready for winter.

Robots used to be naked, but now they're all decked out in fancy clothes, I thought, and at that very moment the child swung around to stare at me. "Don't go making me into a robot," his eyes protested, "because I'm not." Apparently he sensed how much fun I'd had been having, playing with the notion that he was a machine. Clinging to his mother's coat, his neck still twisted around to glare at me, he walked several steps before stumbling and nearly falling. "Be careful where you place your feet," his mother scolded gently. "Why are you always looking behind you?" I detected a slight southern, Swabian lilt in her speech.

I had read in the newspaper about young couples who, having inherited sizable fortunes, were moving from southern Germany to raise their children in this district of Berlin. They were not conservative the way wealthy people were thirty or forty years ago, but a new, green generation. Expensive cars were the sign of older wealthy people, but this new generation, who hated all sorts of cars, rode bicycles instead. While the old guard had feasted on thick steaks, the new wealthy class stuck to their vegetarian diets. All the food they cooked at home was organic and additive-free. Before buying coffee or chocolate, they made sure that the beans had been grown on farms where the workers' rights were respected. This applied to clothing as well, so there'd be a pamphlet detailing the working conditions of everyone involved in the production of, say, a pair of knitted socks. This drove the price up but perhaps gave the buyers the satisfaction of knowing that the more they paid, the greater their contribution toward saving the world.

A "wealthy person" is apparently defined as someone who has enough money so that five generations, including his or her own, can manage without working.

Now about ten yards ahead of me, the boy shook off his mother's hand and started walking backward with both arms stuck out for balance like a tightrope walker. The sidewalk had been shoveled; though bits of snow still stuck to the pavement like sugar, the ice had melted, so there was no danger of him slipping and falling. With high mounds of snow on either side to keep him from wandering out into the street, I suppose you could say the snow was actually keeping him safe. The mother still calmly followed him with her eyes. As a child, I myself had played at walking backward, but that was so long ago I'd forgotten there was such a game. Walking backward, your legs feel as if they don't belong to you. They're sticks—too long, and they only bend at strange angles. I used to wonder if this was what having wooden legs would be like.

Walking backward, you can never shake off the fear

that the back of your head will suddenly bash into something hard. The skin back there gets very sensitive, and your hair rises. When you can't stand not being able to see what's behind you anymore, your skin opens, your hair parts, and a third eye appears.

This mother doesn't yell, "Cut out this foolishness! Come on, we're going," and try to pull her boy along; patiently, she watches him walk backward. With a head full of terms like autonomy, creativity, and the importance of play, she's probably educating her son in his own free private school. There's some sarcasm in this interpretation of mine, but to tell the truth, knowing that my own mother must have had bright yet sad days, days like a deserted field lit by sunlight, has put me in a quandary. From the outside, it's impossible to know all the complicated elements that make up a person's inner feelings. No one can tell what this mother is really thinking, right at this moment. Maybe something terrible has happened, and she's too sad to think about supervising her child's behavior. Or perhaps she's too smitten with him to concentrate on what he's doing. She might secretly be hoping he'll fall down and get what he deserves. Or that she'll be the center of attention if he takes a tumble and starts crying. After all, there are parents like that. Unable to interpret them, children nevertheless remember all their parents' looks, gestures, and words, carrying them on their shoulders like the night sky. Then, when they're old enough to have a couple kids of their own, they put those fragments of memory together as if they were making connections between stars scattered in the sky, forming them into constellations like the Little Dipper or the Great Bear, and, remembering their mothers silently watching them as they walked backward in the snow, they come up with various possibilities as to how she might have felt that day.

Step by step, the boy walked into the endless space behind him. Only children know about these adventures into the unknown, right in the middle of everyday life. I stayed where I was, blocking his path, so he bumped into my stomach and then twisted his head around to look up at me, this time crackling with laughter. He looked happy to have found someone to run into. He certainly wasn't hoping that nothing would stop him, that he'd keep getting farther and farther away from his mother. The moment I felt the warmth of his body, accepting it with the whole of mine, I felt strangely satisfied. I remembered the way children sometimes run toward their mothers, bumping straight into them just for fun, or that game where a group of kids press back to back in a circle knot, and each one tries to push all the others out.

The boy was still dissolved in laughter, but when his mother called his name, he stopped and ran to her, his shoes smacking the pavement. Mother-and-child time, endlessly repeated. Every day they go shopping. Today, and again tomorrow. And countless more times. Infinite repetitions. But not actually infinite, because they will end someday. The end is coming, nearer and nearer.

After the child leaves I am alone, feeling like a child

myself. A child deserted in the middle of town on a snowy day. That's me. If only she would come and take me by the hand. "Let's go shopping," she might say, or "Let's go home and have dinner." If only I had these repetitions to protect me. Then two hands reached out, looking for protection from a strong woman—the hands of a ghost-child wandering the streets. *She* doesn't need me. And I'm fed up with being a child. I want to be someone people can depend on. I had been hunched over like a coward, but now I straighten up, throw out my chest, and stick my elbows out. That very moment my body changes into an Indian teepee, large enough to hold three children. There's no telling when another attack might come. Two of the children huddle together, peering fearfully outside. The third, too young to sense the danger, looks happy, as if this were a game of hide-and-seek. This scene is a sketch by Kathe Kollwitz. The arms of the mother protecting her children look as thick and strong as logs. Like this mother, *she* would probably spread her arms over her daughter and grandchildren if war came, not flinching even if a bomb fell on her shoulders. Stretching a thin vinyl sheet to protect them from sparks would be all I could manage. Or would I be in prison by the time the bombing started, arrested for handing out antiwar pamphlets?

In front of a health food store a man was squatting down to unlock his bicycle when our eyes met. I was sure I'd seen him before. A child about the height of the saddle stood in front of the bike, off to one side. The streetlamp lit up his tearstained face in an odd way, making it look round and bright as the full moon. A child seat was attached to the back of the bike. Actually it was more like a two-wheeled trailer with a green tent on top, big enough for a smallish child of seven. When the snow's piled up, you don't see many bikes with trailers like this. Probably because the mounds of snow on both sides of the road narrowed the bike paths, making navigation more difficult. The man—probably the child's father—was still young and not at all fat; nevertheless, he had a reassuring sort of fatherly fleshiness. I couldn't remember where I had seen him.

"Come on, it's time to go home." The voice sounded strangely sad in the cold air. The child stood there, pouting, refusing to move. "Are you still mad?" the father asked. "I'll buy it for you next time." He reached out for his son's arm, but the boy darted back and hid behind the bike. When the father moved sideways, the boy moved, too. With the bicycle between them, the father couldn't catch his son. "We've got to go home now." This time he tried to trick the boy, taking one step to the right and then swinging back to the left, but the boy, imitating his father's movements perfectly, got away again. "It's getting late." The boy's expression didn't change. "Mama's waiting for us at home." Hearing this, the boy's resistance disappeared like air seeping out of a balloon, and he obediently sat down in his trailer. His blond hair then turned into a prince's crown, his red jacket into a velvet robe, and horses neighed as they pulled the royal carriage through the snow, heading for the palace. I suddenly remembered who the father was.

The left-handed man who worked at the post office, the one who always took my envelopes in his left hand.

Why don't I head for her place where she's preparing a feast for me? The candles are waiting on the table, shedding thick white tears. She invited me over for some delicious venison. She'd never done that before. Unable to conceal my joy, I told her, "I have some boring stuff to do this afternoon, but I won't be late for deer!" And though I checked my watch time and again as I aimlessly wandered the streets, before I knew it I'd headed in the opposite direction from her house and found myself here in Kollwitz Strasse. I can't remember why I came here.

Streams of people seem to be pouring out of the pavement cracks at the south end of Kollwitz Strasse. All have children in tow, both men and women. Though some are couples, most don't have a partner with them, so one parent must be shopping while the other is busy elsewhere. A whole crowd of parents and children is swallowed up into the open doors to a large organic food store. I follow them in and see that most are gathered around the bakery counter near the entrance. Some are picking out bread while others drink coffee or tea, and still others eye the cakes lined up in the glass case.

Just then, I felt someone touch my hand from behind. I turned around to see the ghost-child. Looking up at me, he took me by the hand and pulled me toward the back of the shop. Being a ghost, his hand wasn't exactly warm, but not so cold that I wanted to let go.

"There's something you should buy for me," the

ghost announced confidently, as if this were well within his rights.

"You want me to buy you something even though you're dead?" I thought of asking as a joke but then, considering how cruel "even though you're dead" would sound to someone who really was dead, decided not to. After all, this child might have been so poor no one had ever bought him anything while he was alive, which might be why he'd come back as a ghost.

"What do you want?"

"Negro's kisses."

That had definitely been the name of a cheap sweet a long time ago, but the name had been changed because "Negro" was now a racist word. Egg whites whipped into a cream ball about the size of a child's fist, covered with a thin layer of chocolate. Unable to remember the new name, I said, "*Negro* is a word you use when you're looking down on someone with black skin, so why don't we just stop using it, okay?" It was no use telling this sort of thing to a dead boy, but with a child standing in front of me, I always want to explain about words.

"Why would you want somebody you look down on to kiss you?" he asked—quite the comeback.

Without thinking, almost automatically I answered, "Lots of people who look down on women want kisses from them, don't they?" This bit of knowledge would do him no good at all. "Here they are—chocolate kisses." I carefully pronounced the new name. On the back of the box it said that the chocolate was from Bolivia, grown on a farm where the laborers were never forced to work more than thirty-five hours a week but were still paid enough to support a family of eight, and that the eggs were from free-range chickens who hadn't ingested any antibiotics or chemically enhanced grain. But seeing how the phrase "family of eight" on the back echoed the "box of eight" on the front, I wondered if racism wasn't peeping out like a bad joke from somewhere I never would have expected to find it.

Oblivious to these thoughts of mine, the ghost grabbed the box of chocolate kisses and tossed it into a cart, the hint of a smile on his pale face. His eyes were sunken, and the skin beneath his nose was much too dry and wrinkly for one so young. Gripping the side of the shopping cart, he gawked around. His arms were so thin they didn't seem to be attached to his shoulders, and under his caved-in chest, his stomach stuck out. Definitely not a child of this age. He desperately searched the shelves for sweets he knew. He probably couldn't have cared less about the hundreds of rich new candies lining the shelves. Ghosts, it seemed, did not devote themselves to devouring the future. All this child wanted was to recover another thread that had slipped from his grasp during his very slender life.

Such a lot of candy in a health food store. I'd assumed that this health-conscious generation wouldn't even consider buying cheap sweets, but clearly I was wrong. Apparently there were plenty of people who, rather than give up sweets, enthusiastically looked for ways to make them healthy. I saw gummy bears, but they were all brown. They had animal crackers too. "Buy

me some sweets," the ghost said. "Buy me frozen dogs."
I looked for the sweets called "frozen dogs," layers of
biscuit and cream covered with chocolate, and there
they were. Of course they bore the inevitable "organic"
and "free trade" labels. His brow furrowed, the boy was
desperately trying to remember more kinds of sweets. I
was about to say, "If you eat too much you'll get sick,"
but didn't. This child was a ghost. He was already dead.
There was no use worrying about a dead child getting
sick. Apparently not realizing he was dead, he said, "If
I get sick I can go to the doctor. Dr. Kollwitz will see
me even if I don't have any money." Kathe Kollwitz's
husband was a doctor, and the waiting room at his clinic
was always full of poor people. She sometimes drew
sketches of them. Which meant that this ghost must
have lived in Berlin a century before and had perhaps
emerged from one of her sketches.

"Have you been to see Dr. Kollwitz?"

"Sure, lots of times."

"And what did he say?"

"He told me to eat more good things. Let's buy fried
sausages!"

"I don't think they sell them here. How about fish
sticks—do you like them?" Fish sticks are rectangles
of fried white fish. Even now kids like them, but since
they only went on sale after the war maybe this boy
has never seen them. They don't look like fish and
hardly taste like it either, which might explain their
popularity. A sort of junk food, you might say, but with
good enough ingredients they wouldn't be so different

from fried fish. Probably much better for him than fried sausages, I thought, like a mother worrying about her child's health, which seemed strange even to me. Would anyone adopt a ghost? I was about to buy some when I saw how much they cost and discovered that they were way out of my price range.

"They're awfully expensive," I said. "Hang on a minute, there's some important information on the back of the box." To buy some time, I started to read. *You want everything in your life to be 100% natural. But you still want the fish sticks you loved as a child, and you want your children to enjoy them too. These fish sticks are the creation of a young man who, with this very dream in his heart, rented a section of the Mekong River, where for twenty years he organically raised Mekong giant catfish, which he fried in flour made from wheat grown with absolutely no fertilizers or chemical additives.* Strangely enough, as I read I started to feel that these fish sticks were truly a work of art, so even at this price they might be worth it.

"Come on, buy me some."

"They cost an awful lot, don't you think? After all, they're just fish sticks."

"But you've got money, don't you?"

"I'm not rich, you know—not at all."

"But you've got enough with you now, so why keep looking for something cheaper?"

What a cheeky ghost. I saw something round and yellow reflected in the glass. Taking a closer look, I saw it was a melon. The green was zucchini, and the white was the sweater worn by the woman who stood beside the melon, staring at it. The glass didn't reflect anything that was too small or not brightly colored. Wondering if I could see myself, I tried standing on tiptoe and leaning over to one side. I'd heard that ghosts are not reflected in mirrors, but what about someone shopping with a ghost?

I was thinking up excuses in case the ghost asked me to buy him a melon, but he wasn't interested. Perhaps there weren't any melons in Berlin a hundred years ago. Since this area was East Germany, you probably couldn't even have bought bananas here until 1989. Yet now it looked like a painting of the tropics, with colorful oranges, grapefruits, lemons, persimmons, kumquats, and pineapples, all in a row. With orchards on the other side of the globe being rented to grow fruit organically, tropical fruits were available even in the winter. Though he didn't seem to notice the grapefruits and pineapples, the boy stopped in front of a mountain of apples and, picking out a bright red one about the size of his fist, carefully put it into the cart. The shopping cart was big enough to hold a baby, but all we had in it so far were one box of eight chocolate kisses, a package of frozen dogs and another with a dozen fish sticks, and this one small apple.

Letting go of the cart, the boy grabbed the hem of my coat and dragged me over to the cereal section. A middle-aged man, graying at the temples, was holding an ocher-colored box of cereal, intently reading the explanation on the back. That culture—I saw it in the design on the box. That culture ... The name was caught somewhere in the back of my throat and wouldn't come out. When I tried to recover it, the words "Asuka Culture" rose up in my mind, blocking the way.

"Buy me that," the ghost demanded, pointing at the box in the man's hand. The man looked down at him and smiled, then strolled over to the wine section. I picked up the box he'd returned to the shelf and began reading the explanation on the back.

"Buy it for me."

"Wait till I finish reading this." *The people who consumed this grain in the mountains of Peru five thousand years ago regarded it as a sacred food and probably heated it over the fire, as they cooked rice. Because we have processed it like popcorn, it can be added to salad just as it is or mixed with cereal.* The name I'd forgotten came back to me. *Aztec.* In my mind, the "t" disappeared, changing it to "Asuka."

"Come on, buy me a box."

"Do you know what this is?"

"Sure—it's quinoa," he answered casually.

How did he know that? My cereal-like brain, doused with milk and stirred with a spoon, was rich in minerals, but still I was growing more and more confused.

"Have you ever eaten that?" a voice suddenly asked. I looked up to see that the man from before was back, carrying a bottle of wine in one hand. I wondered for a moment if he might not be a ghost, too. Though not as white as the boy's, his cheeks were definitely pale, his eyes red around the rims. "I can't decide whether to buy a box or not," he went on. "I've just come from a world where there's nothing to buy, so I'm overwhelmed by all this merchandise." He ran his index finger over his forehead. At that moment, tall spears of yellow grain shimmered around his shoulders. A world where there's nothing to buy—could that be prison? Or perhaps some North African city under siege? Maybe he had leukemia and had been in hospital for a long time. There are plenty of places on Earth that aren't flooded with things for sale.

"The box is a pretty color, don't you think?" he said, coming at me from a completely different angle. "Orange, like the sun peeking out from between the clouds." He went on, "Its warmth reminds you of the earth, its fragility, of delicate flowers."

"It's the very color of South America—that's probably why they chose it."

"You mean Aztec, Inca, Maya?"

"That's right. The history of this grain apparently goes back a lot further, though."

"It that right? I've been cut off from the outside world for so long I don't know much about things like that."

I smiled at him in spite of myself. His face crinkled up into a mass of wrinkles as if he were trying to smile back, but his eyes still looked sad. The ghost-child, finding all this terribly boring, braced himself as he pulled at my hand, then let go when I didn't move and marched over to a nearby shelf where he grabbed box after box of twenty-five teabags each until he couldn't hold any more. Leaving the cart, I ran over to him and scolded,

"Stop that! You can't just take things off the shelf that you're not going to buy." The scolding apparently made him feel a little relieved. He didn't seem likely to demand that I buy him all that tea, but too poorly coordinated to use his right hand to return the boxes stacked up on his left arm to the shelf, he ended up dropping them all. One by one they hit the floor with a dry, rustling sound. Boxes with strange names, like Green Energy, Woman's Brew, and Breath Tea scattered all over the floor. Each piece of merchandise he dropped would broaden his world a little more. He would move on from there, not by buying things but by dropping them. There should be room for this sort of customer too. Purchases alone—things he wanted or things he had to have—wouldn't help a ghost at all. I myself had no reason for being in this store in the first place. Or to be spending time on this street, for that matter. She had invited me for dinner, so why didn't I head straight for the subway stop? I'd be in time if I left right away. Before I knew it the man from before was squatting down beside me, helping me put the boxes of tea back on the shelf. That cheeky ghost-child was hanging onto his shoulders, grinning. A woman in her sixties stopped to smile down at the man and whisper, "I envy you, shopping with your family." Flustered, I stood up and shook my head hard from side to side as if to shake off a bad dream. This brought white powder floating down, which I thought with a start must be dandruff, but when I looked at the floor I saw feathers. Astonished, I shook my head again and more feathers fell. Had I become a crane? A crane who had turned into a woman, had a human family, and was now shopping with them as if nothing was out of the ordinary. Opening my wallet at the checkout counter I looked up at my reflection in the glass and saw that I was indeed a crane. A crane who used her beak to pluck feathers from her own breast, which immediately turned into euros.

I was not a crane. Soft, tiny feathers were escaping one by one through the seams of my down jacket. The moment they slip through the tiny holes, the feathers are thinner than silk thread, but once outside, they're plump and fluffy again. Perhaps there are seams between the present and the future, with tiny holes in them through which people go back and forth.

Although I'd opened my wallet, I passed through the checkout counter without buying anything and outside found that the city had turned into a black-and-white picture. The ocher of the outside walls of the buildings and the emerald green of the cars were now wavering between black and white, having lost their colors and been absorbed into a spectrum of gray.

With this black-and-white scene before me, I no longer knew what era I was living in. I was surrounded by a group of children. They were all holding out bowls, begging with their eyes for food. Certain that if they looked away for even a second they wouldn't get their share, they never took their eyes off me. The bowls were white as bone inside. Their roundness perfectly matched the round faces of the children. The children disappeared the moment I realized that this was a picture: the famous poster Kathe Kollwitz created during the 1920s to tell the world about starving children. There's not one unnecessary line, so her message comes straight at you. But perhaps the image of hungry children didn't have such a clear message for the world back then. The word "hunger" probably didn't even occur to passersby who saw them shuffling along, their shoulders drawn in, or sitting by the road, their thin arms hugging their knees. Individual characteristics erased from their faces, these children were arranged for the greatest effect, each one given the same bowl. Their names were replaced by a single category: "German children." Artists are also artistic directors, with a hint of the liar about them, and their lies worry me so much that I can never bring myself to take action, and so become quite useless.

Sometimes when you walk by a window you get a glimpse of what's going on inside the house. A man stands by the door, hanging his head. His wife and children look at him, their eyes full of hope, but maybe he lost his job today. He stands there, staring down at the floor. The situation in the house next door seems just as bleak. The father must have been killed in the war, for the photograph of him in his uniform is draped with a black ribbon. The mother, her eyes half-closed in anguish, presses her head into the pillow. Until the day before yesterday she'd managed, by helping clear away the rubble, to earn just enough money to keep her children fed somehow, but now she has a high fever and can't get out of bed. Her little children stand by her bedside. They don't know what to do.

I quickened my pace, heading for the park.

As it was already dark, no children were playing anymore, but I saw an old woman sitting on a bench, her
right hand across her forehead as she stared out at the
city. Snow had fallen on her head, turning her hair white.
The shawl over her shoulders, too, was pure white. She
wasn't wearing a coat. The skirt wrapped around her
lower body was thick as carpet, and she had big boots
on. Assuming she was a homeless woman sitting there
on the bench, people walked by without speaking to her.
But I couldn't help noticing how extraordinary her face
was—the strong ridge of her eyebrows, and the determination in the eyes beneath, looking straight ahead.

"You drew those pictures, didn't you?" I said. "Of
poverty that individuals can't help."

Kathe Kollwitz apparently didn't hear me, for she
sat there, frozen, staring off into space. Perhaps she
was remembering how she had sent her younger son
to war, to his death. A draft notice had come for the
older boy, but his brother, still too young, needn't have
gone. He had insisted, though, saying, "I want to fight
to protect our homeland," and Kollwitz couldn't hide
her joy at hearing this son, once a pampered child, now
talking like a grown man. Sensing his mother's pride,
the boy again declared his intention to go, even as his
father tried to stop him. His mother should have taken
her husband's side and refused to let him go. Not only
to protect him from the danger; she should have taught
him that war is never for the sake of the homeland. The
sight of German and French boys of the same age, next-
door neighbors, shooting and killing each other was too

sad for comedy and too ridiculous for tragedy. And some were killed by their own country's bombs, while others starved to death when their army's food supply was cut off. All the lies about France being on the verge of invading Germany had been so transparent that looking back, she can't see why she was stupid enough to believe them.

Kollwitz sat motionless, her right hand, big as a baseball mitt, covering half her face. She castigated herself for killing her own son, the shame and pain growing so strong she could hardly breathe. The sun would set, the moon rise and disappear, and the horizon would lighten again: if she sat here long enough, her body would turn to stone. As she gradually turned to stone, the pain subsided, little by little. She would stay here until the process was complete. But as her entire body was about to change, she stood up, took a hammer in her hand, and started pounding on her own shoulders, the sound ringing in the air. The stone crumbled, exposing the human skin underneath. Round shoulders, round elbows, a smooth line from wrist to hand, and a single thought flowing from the heart down to her fingertips, which brought the searing pain back. Kollwitz wailed, clawing at her breast and striking her forehead on the ground. She held her son, now cold, on her knees, leaning over and trying to warm him with her own body heat. Pressing her ear to her dead son's chest, she waited patiently for the heartbeat that would never come. Looking up at the heavens she howled and cried until she grew hoarse, but even after her voice had given out, her whole body continued to shake. If only she could become a sculpture. Though she had produced many drawings and prints, she had known that she was meant to be a sculptor since her youth. And now, the only way to escape this pain was to become a sculpture herself.

When she came to her senses, she had become a statue of Mary, lovingly holding the body of Christ after he had been taken down from the cross. Mary was not responsible for Christ's death. After he was crucified, all she could do was shower him with endless, unconditional love. By becoming Mary, Kathe Kollwitz was finally able to stop condemning herself. On the other hand, as Mary she would no longer be performing the unique act of one individual, but might be dismissed with a single word, such as "Pietà."

Startled, I came to myself. This was no time to be criticizing other people. If I dawdled here much longer, the venison she was cooking would get cold. I headed back toward the subway station. If I hurried, I would probably be in time.

MAJAKOWSKIRING

The German word *Strasse* can refer to various kinds of streets—some are straight, others twist and turn, and still others divide into two. Some are dead ends, while others are very long, and change their names many times along the way. Once in a while a street forms a circle, in which case it's not a *Strasse*, but a *Ring*. A *Ring* can also refer to an engagement ring. And Wagner's "Der Ring des Nibelungen" cycle is sometimes called the Ring for short—before you know it, a tiny ring has grown into a huge cycle. And the ring that symbolized the bond between two people is now large enough to encompass the saga of an entire family.

After the wall around a castle town is destroyed, the modern street constructed where it once stood becomes a very large *Ring*. The Vienna Ringstrasse, for example, encircling the central part of the city, has lots of trolley stops on it. Majakowskiring, on the other hand, is so small you can walk all the way around it in about seven minutes.

When you leave the main street and enter this *Ring*, the traffic sounds completely disappear and all is quiet. Then your tympanic membrane begins to catch the chirping of birds until before you know it your ears are full of birdsong and you forget there even was a main street as air from the large park opposite, stretching out like a forest, gradually enters your lungs. There's a castle in the park, and lots of trees taller than church spires—here, there, and everywhere. Trees, trees, trees, *Bäume, Bäume, Bäume*! While I'd like to stroll around this park for a bit, I still have things left to do back in Majakowskiring, so at least until I remember what those things were, I'll stay here in the *Ring*, walking around it.

I was like a nun walking slowly down the corridors of a convent. I firmly believed that after several trips around the courtyard I'd find the answer. But without a sacred text to recollect, I wasn't really a nun.

There were neither shops nor people, only a kitten that crawled under a fence and, rolling out on my side of it, came over to play with my shoelaces. I looked down to see they were untied. The pure white kitten was fluffier than a cotton ball, and its tail was dancing as if it were a separate being. Rather than tying my shoelaces, I lifted my foot and circled it around. Delighted, the kitten kept on playing. Then another kitten, white like the first, crawled under the fence and started playing too—but with its sibling's tail, not with my shoelaces. The first kitten twisted around and raised its short forelegs. Still another kitten slid under the fence—another sibling, no doubt. This one was apparently shy, for it simply watched the others play, making no attempt to join them until it was butted from behind by a fourth kitten and thrown straight into the melee. The fifth and sixth appeared shoulder to shoulder, competing to see who could get through faster. Their mother never came.

All six were white all over, maybe because they were purebreds, a word that brings Nazi ideology to mind and is therefore no longer in use regarding humans; nevertheless, there are still people who think nothing of applying it to cats, which seems frightening and terribly cruel.

Suddenly all six kittens stopped moving and pricked up their ears, and a split second later they all took off in the same direction. They must have picked up some sound I couldn't hear. Hurrying after them, I eventually found myself standing in front of a large restaurant rumored to have gone out of business a while back. Though I couldn't remember the name, it was definitely something strange like "Rest House for Comedians."

The spacious front garden was dotted with bushes, among which were several tables, and to the back of the garden was an elegant wooden villa. Its door was open, under a "Welcome" sign, so those rumors must have been incorrect, and since they'd made me wish I'd come here with her before it closed, this was a relief.

But then I had a terrible thought. Maybe I'd slipped back in time, back to when the restaurant was still in business. That would be really awful—if I were now on a different path from the one I'd taken, my fate would change, and she and I might never meet. Maybe I'd end up with someone else altogether, though perhaps that would be better, after all. If I were to ask that other person, "How about a coffee on Majakowskiring?" instead of putting me off with excuses like, "Why go so far for a cup of coffee?" or "I'd like to but I'm busy at work these days," she might just come to the restaurant at the time we'd decided on, where she'd sit across from me while enjoyed our coffee, smiling, her eyes narrowing with delight as we chatted about things that were far from here, people who were elsewhere, or faraway countries. She might have the same sort of fondness for East Berlin as me, or perhaps she'd be much bigger, so huge that when she leaned way back in this armchair called Berlin her head would touch Poland, and if she yawned and stretched her fingertips would reach into Russia.

Not that I mean to compare the two, but the woman I'm with now never reaches out any farther than she has to. While carefully guarding her own territory, keeping it under control, she's never curious enough to invade anyone else's.

If I asked her to have coffee with me on Majakowski-ring, she'd probably give me a "Why would you go all the way to Pankow just for coffee?" sort of look. Then, figuring that maybe I liked Mayakovsky's poetry, she'd blurt out, "You go ahead and wait for me—I'll come later if I finish my work in time." But she wouldn't finish.

Though as a student she saw the Berlin Wall from the western side every day, she was always facing toward the west. A typical West Berliner, she sometimes visited her parents, who lived in Munich, but always spent her summer vacations in Tuscany, or on Mallorca, or at La Palma, never even considering Krakow or Odessa.

I want to go east and north. Here in Pankow I'm already in the northeastern part of Berlin, but I want to go farther east, farther north. If I wasn't always worrying about what she might think, I might be able to go farther.

Now I've been carried back to a fatal turning point and am shaking the dice in my sweaty hand. If I choose a separate path, my fate and hers will never cross. Then I'll be able to go as far as I like, without waiting or worrying about how she'll take it. I can leave Berlin. Or even the FRG, for that matter. Throwing off the repressive obi I've had wrapped around my body, I want to go far, far away, with nothing to hold me back.

But perhaps I would be unable to forget her even after my fate had changed, and find myself so haunted by memories that I'd end up storming into her house, saying, "You may think you don't know me but you're wrong—if only you'd turned the corner on that street one block up we would have met," offering explanations she couldn't understand.

Or what if the opposite happened? If one day the bell were to ring and I opened the door to find her standing there looking exhausted, just back from the future? Of course, she would be a stranger to me. "We were married for fifteen years," she'd say, "but just now I was pulled back twenty years into the past and chose a different path from the one I'd been on. That's why we're strangers now. You probably don't remember me, but I know you." Though hearing her say that would definitely be upsetting, and no matter how long I stared at her I doubt I'd feel any love for her.

The city is full of people you might have met, who might have become close friends. Maybe that's why, even when I'm with an old friend, someone I feel close to, I can't help suspecting that there are plenty of other people around I would have enjoyed being with just as much, if only I'd had the chance to meet them. That's why I make a point of referring to the person I've been with—sharing bed and bread—for twenty years as "her," and why I make arrangements for us to have one more chance of meeting in the labyrinth of the city, hoping to discover her again for the very first time. I want to meet her in a coffee shop, where we'll stir the sugar in our coffee with rapid movements, as if we only have time for one cup, savoring this time together, knowing we may never meet again, looking into each other's faces again and again as we sip our coffee. And even if we always eat at home, I want to dress up and buy her a bouquet as if she'd invited me over.

Walking down a street lined with other people's houses, I feel light and breezy. If I notice that one of those warm, quiet terracotta roof tiles has started to crumble, I needn't check my bank account and start planning to have the roof repaired. If the Polish Cultural Center seems deserted, I don't have to come up with ingenious ideas for making it more popular. If the grounds of the Chinese Embassy are overgrown with weeds, I'm not the one who has to clear them away. And I can stand right in front of the house where Johan Becher once lived and, without having read a single one of his poems, not feel the slightest bit guilty. An afternoon stroll is never quite so luxurious as when you're totally unnecessary to your surroundings.

But once in a while a building will catch my eye. I simply have to go inside. The entrance looks like a mysterious initial that I can't help staring at. Like a wary cat, I softly lift the soles of my feet as I enter. The balance scale inside my head goes off-kilter, moving wildly up and down, and though the floor seemed solid enough when I tested it with the toe of my shoe, inside my body, the bits that were supposed to be heavy were so light they floated up, while the light bits sunk heavily.

Inside, the restaurant was dimly lit and perfectly quiet. That same old picture of Mayakovsky was hanging on the wall. The first time I saw it here I thought with a start that it might be a spirit photograph.

Although Mayakovsky did come to Berlin a number of times, he had no special relationship to this street. But then the street was named after him, along with its restaurant with his photograph on display, and as the customers looked up at it, talking about him as they sipped their coffee, perhaps his ghost heard the name and came to haunt the place. Ghosts apparently don't come back to this world unless there's a special place for them here. Marx's spirit haunts Karl-Marx-Strasse, and Kant's appears in Kantstrasse. There are so many streets named after Goethe that his ghost gets awfully confused and rarely manages to haunt any of them. But Mayakovsky would undoubtedly come straight here. There'd apparently once been a square named after him in Russia, but even ghosts are avoiding Russia now. I've heard that if someone happens to read a dead poet's work as criticism of the current regime, his ghost is sometimes arrested. That must be why Russian poets are tearfully abandoning their native land to gather in Berlin.

I stared at Mayakovsky's face in the photograph. He looks as if he was dragged out of bed while dead drunk, placed in handcuffs, and slammed against the wall for a mugshot. Looking slightly upward, he glowers at the camera, wary but not frightened, wearing what looks like a loose-fitting rubashka tunic. He has an irresistible charisma that reminds me of David Bowie. Being a photograph, he couldn't be giving off an aroma, yet my nostrils are tickled just the same. My eyes dart quickly over the surface, searching for the source of that fragrance. Erotic charm is tangled in his hair, tousled from sleep. His eyes, angry yet lonely, come nearer and nearer, making me want to hug him.

"I'll be there at 4:00, Maria said," murmurs Mayakovski. "8:00, 9:00, 10:00." 11:00, 12:00, 13:00, I count silently, picking up where he left off. 14:00, 15:00, 16:00, I used to wait for her for hours. 17:00, 18:00, 19:00, but no matter how long I waited, she never came. If I waited at home I'd be sure to catch her, but I wanted her to come to me, at a faraway place I'd taken time to get to. 20:00, 21:00, 22:00.

What if I kept on counting, past 23:00, beyond that terrifying border of 24:00—midnight. If I missed the chance to return to zero, I'd have to keep on traveling alone into nonexistent hours, 25:00, 26:00, 27:00, and then I'd have no one to share time with.

"I'll be there at 4:00," Maria said. "8:00, 9:00, 10:00,"

Mayakovsky repeated. I know that painful, empty feeling of waiting for someone who doesn't come, I was going to say, but my tongue had other ideas and, before I knew it, came out with something entirely different:

"How long are you going to wait? You have a different future, don't you?"

That sounded awfully affected. The word *Zukuft* (future) left a residue of falsehood on my tongue. Why had I spoken to Mayakovsky in German anyway? That sort of thing often happens in dreams—you find yourself conversing in a language the other person doesn't know. I've heard that while Mayakovsky was in New York, he became very close to a Russian exile named Elli, who translated poems from German for him. Their translational trysts led to insemination and produced a new female poet, which means Mayakovsky didn't know German. Or was he just feigning ignorance so he'd have an excuse to get close to Elli?

"I want it now—that future you're talking about." Mayakovsky was excited, his breaths coming quickly as if he couldn't wait another minute.

"Don't get so antsy," I replied as calmly as I could. "You've got plenty of time, haven't you?" But then I realized how cruel that must have sounded. After all, he might have taken it to mean, "Being dead, you have all the time in the world."

Imagining the future is a mental exercise I've practiced since I was a child. "What do you think the capitals of civilized countries will look like a hundred years from now?" Since my fifth-grade art teacher first asked me this question, I've redrawn my vision of the future again and again. Every time I try to imagine a city in the future, the screen in my brain goes blank, making it hard to breathe. Bearing the pain, I regulate my breathing and gradually begin to see things. These visions are often based on strange-looking buildings that actually exist. For instance, the Reichstag Building, which has a dome surrounded by a glass wall, with a spiral passage that follows the curve from the dome's base all the way to the top. As they climb the slope, German citizens, immigrants, and tourists can all watch the politicians at work through the glass. It's something like an aquarium. Some of the spectators cheer, "Glasnost!" When you reach the very top of the dome, you look straight down on the politicians' crowns, many of which are crooked. You can watch corruption as it happens. It's more thrilling than a live broadcast. The politicians, on the other hand, don't stop their dirty dealings just because they're being watched; when they are exposed, they'll freely admit their transgressions and bow their heads low. "I apologize from the bottom of my heart to the German people," they might say, without seeming to feel much responsibility. That's because "the German people" are just like customers, so they don't mind bowing down before them at all as long as they can make money off them.

There are no cars in the center of the city. The Reichstag, the prime minister's residence, and the House of the World's Cultures are all connected by a river called the Spree, with pleasure boats going back and forth. On deck, to the sound of clinking beer glasses, tourists chat with members of parliament. The boat makes a stop in front of an island with museums of art and history, looming like a row of castles. You open the front door of an art museum and enter a huge hall with a high ceiling where homeless people live in huts they have built themselves. From the darkness behind their shanties, Rembrandt peers out as if to say, "Can you see me from there?" Though Cézanne's apples are laughing merrily, no one reaches out to take one and bite into it. In the historical museum next door, children are playing with primitive stone tools. There's no need to worry that guards will come running and scream, "You mustn't touch the artifacts on exhibit!" The thousands of excavated objects, so long sleeping in storage, have been set free and given to the children. On the walls of Catholic churches, photographs of Muslims at prayer are on display. At City Hall, visitors listen as a man with a beard, dressed as a woman, politely explains about certificates of residence. Lines of demonstrators march slowly from embassy to embassy. Uniformed policemen join them as they shout antinuclear-power slogans. Looking carefully at the clouds floating by, you see that they all have human faces. No one ever uses words like "imagination" or "creativity" anymore. People are now expected to use their brains in imaginative and creative ways as a matter of course, and these two forces have begun to move politics. Is this the sort of future Mayakovsky had in mind? A city

like a museum of modern art, where you can shake off
the anxiety of living just by taking a walk?

But wandering aimlessly through the center of town
would only make her feel more anxious. Every day, as
if repeating a prayer, she says she wants to buy an old
farmhouse in northern Brandenburg, on the border
between the plains and forest. That's why she works
from morning until night, saving up her money little by
little. She thinks people who stroll around town, spending money on coffee or cake or the movies, are wasting
their lives.

When I'm looking out on fields from a farmhouse window or walking through the forest, I don't really think
of words. Though the word *Baum* comes to mind when
I see a tree, I couldn't tell you whether it was an oak or
a beech. The chirping of birds tells me that *Vögel* are
somewhere near, but whether they're angry thrushes or
robins making love is beyond me. I do know the words
for various kinds of birds. *Amsel,* for instance, or *Rot-
kehlchen.* But because I only know them from poems, I
don't connect them to a bird with a red head, or to that
black bird pecking at a worm by the side of the road.
The words go fluttering through space, while the birds
perched in the trees ignore them. That words really
have no relation to the world gives me a strange, empty
sort of feeling.

The city is just like the inside of my brain: the words
on shop signs create endless waves of associations—the
chattering of passersby grows into an opera, travelers

scatter foreign words on museum floors, wars carved in stone send out continuous warnings, drunks in the subway make campaign speeches, and in coffee shops, the people at the next table are always putting on a play with an indecipherable plot, as teas and cakes with tea-and-cake–like names go into mouths and down gullets to be digested in stomachs, while money moves from wallets to checkout counters, from companies to banks, and, without learning to add, people keep getting older, as year after year is added to their ages.

The city is an amusement park of the senses, a rehearsal for a revolution, a restaurant serving up loneliness, a workshop for words. Surrounded by city scenes that look like the future, you believe you'll soon be able to grasp the future itself. This is especially true when you're intensely, violently waiting for someone, because there's the fact that even if you meet the awaited person at the appointed time, you will still have the days after that to endure, and that never occurs to you, that you still have all this time to live through, slowly, stoically, moment after moment. You want everything all at once, right now. You're not afraid of being hurt. You'll embrace her with your entire body. If she pushes you away, you can quickly step aside. There's no need for pain—no matter how many times you're rejected, there are new chances for happiness waiting everywhere in the city streets.

Mayakovsky's cheeks are red, and his eyes glitter. Maybe he has a high fever. "I spent all night writing a bouquet of ten thousand rose words and gave them all to

Lilya the next morning," he says. "But Lilya threw my roses on the floor and screamed, 'If you want to write go ahead, you can grow old buried in these scrap-paper poems of yours,' and then laughed at me, a wild sort of laugh."

"Anyone would naturally reject roses that were forced on them that way," I replied. "People have an instinctive urge to protect their own territory, you know."

"So what should I have done?"

"Why not try slowing down the flow of time until you can't tell whether you're waiting or not? Or try walking so slowly you forget who you're going to meet? Besides," I started to say and then stopped myself. Mayakovsky was already sneering. This must have sounded awfully cowardly to him. Dilute your desire to meet someone to one-tenth, one-twentieth, one-fortieth of its original intensity, until your heart reaches the point where not meeting her and meeting her feel the same. That way there's no need to worry about falling into despair. Definitely the coward's way out.

Be that as it may, it was very odd for Mayakovsky to be standing there, behind glass. Since he was a photograph, I guess it couldn't be helped. Whether he resided in a two-dimensional or a three-dimensional world wasn't clear. Determined to find out which, I stepped forward for a closer look, but the face looking back at me from behind the glass was one I'd never seen before. It wasn't the face of the poet, but my own, reflected in the glass. A human face, eyelashes fluttering, lips slightly parted, apparently breathing with difficulty. There was no one here besides me.

Loneliness descended like a chill, straight down my spine. The poet had never been here in the first place. I crumpled down into a seat by the window in this deserted restaurant and waited for a waiter who would never come. I drew my finger across the table, covered with a thin layer of dust; the light from the window caught the trail of my fingertip, making only that place shine as if wet. Hearing a loud click I turned around, but the door at the back was closed. If that door were to suddenly swing open, who would walk in? I imagined her coming toward me, and at that moment, feeling warm, moist breath on my cheek, I looked up with a start. Mayakovsky was sitting beside me. Utterly impossible, but here he was.

"The door opens, and he appears," Mayakovsky mumbled.

"No, he won't. You're just wishing he would."

"The door opens, and he appears."

"Who appears?"

"A man named Osip, a close friend of mine who's also Lilya's husband. Osip, Lilya, and I were three. We weren't fooling around on the sly. We didn't hide anything. We opened our hearts to each other, then stood in a circle, our arms around each other's shoulders, and cried out loud. And in the end, we swore to spend our lives loving each other."

"So that was your futuristic project."

"But it didn't work out. When there are three, one person is always a third wheel."

"What made you fall in love with a married woman? Was it *the sorrows of young Werther*, maybe?" I'd meant this to sound light and teasing, but my voice came out terribly serious.

"I probably wanted to free her from the trap of her bourgeois life. But there was a contradiction in this desire of mine. I was aware of it myself. I believe it was her physical warmth and the sense of security she gave off that attracted me in the first place. She was the sort of person who, no matter how upset she was, would never go out, get blind drunk, and then fall down and freeze to death in the street. She was never going to ask me to commit suicide with her. But then again, maybe she was only able to keep that sense of warmth and stability because she was protected by bourgeois society. That's a contradiction, wouldn't you say?"

"But she herself wasn't satisfied with that stable life, was she?"

"She had apparently been suffering from insomnia. There was nothing specific she was dissatisfied with, but even so she was always irritated, feeling she couldn't go on with her bourgeois life. That was when we met. Lilya thought she had found something in me that was lacking in her husband. But he was a close friend of mine. A friend as important as a lover. Besides, she never considered divorcing him. She didn't have the slightest intention of leaving him to wander the streets with me and me alone. And so the three of us decided to live together."

"It's amazing you could be so practical."

"But each time the door opened and the third person entered the room, the whole thing fell apart."

This all sounded to me like a play. The door opens, and someone comes in. That's enough to make a drama. You don't need a story. Without anyone being unfaithful, or in love with two people, or breaking up: all it takes is the door opening and the entrance of a third person for the drama to begin. A violent argument ensues—its content doesn't matter much. One of the three leaves. Nobody really cares what happens to the two who are left behind. Perhaps they'll get a pineapple out of the refrigerator, cut it in slices which they'll line up neatly on a plate, and eat them with a silver fork as they sit on the sofa watching television. Pineapple is *Ananas* in German, and I believe it's also called that in Russian. A while ago I went to a vegetable shop run by a Russian who was talking excitedly with a customer. *Ananas, Ananas.* The anarchist's *Ananas*, Anna Karenina's *Ananas*. Only the pineapple was labeled ананас, in the Cyrillic alphabet. If I forced her to read it, she might get it wrong and pronounce it "ahahak." When she sees something written in Russian, she never bothers to ask how the letters are pronounced. She has no interest in reading Russian in the first place.

The bourgeois couple eating pineapple in their living room no longer need an audience. And when the audience goes home, they'll find the same sort of pineapple and the same kind of sofa waiting for them—so why pay for tickets to see their own everyday lives on the stage? Their gaze shifts from the couple left alone in their living room to the third person who has left the room. From here on in it's not a play but a movie. The camera follows the man outside. He hurries down a dark street barely lit by street lamps to board the trolley car, which he rides for two stops before getting off and going into a bar, where he gulps a glass of clear liquid, noisily slaps some coins down on the counter, and goes back out again to pound on the door of an artist friend's atelier; then, finding that his friend is out, he slips around to the back entrance to the theater, where there's a guard who won't let him in. There's nothing for him to do but lie down on a park bench.

"We live in terrible times," Mayakovsky murmurs. "This is no time to sit at home eating pineapple. You have to go out."

As he speaks, Mayakovsky wraps his broad, gray muffler around and around his neck. I meant to laugh and tell him jokingly that if he kept wrapping that muffler around his neck it would look like he wanted to hang himself, but suddenly I lost my voice. A moment ago he'd been talking about lost love and pineapples, and now he was going on about "terrible times" and politics. Conversations about fruit always lead into political topics. In the socialist bloc of Europe, there wasn't ever enough coffee or bananas. Pineapples must have been in short supply, too. So whether or not this pineapple shortage indicates a low standard of living is naturally something we need to discuss. Then there's the inevitable emergence of a social class with easy access to hard-to-get products—we need to consider why this privileged class always stands out most strikingly in societies where shortages are the gravest problem.

Somewhere in the distance, there was an explosion. I was about to down the rest of my *Brombeere* (raspberry) juice in one gulp and run outside when I realized there was no juice glass on the table. The waiter had never come. This restaurant wasn't even open. It had gone out of business after all. Then, I remembered it was summer. Yet Mayakovsky was dressed for winter with a heavy coat and a scarf. He had apparently disappeared while I wasn't watching. When had he left? If I hurried, I might catch him.

The *Ring* named after him was deserted and perfectly still. Wondering if he had left the *Ring* I went out to the main street, where I caught sight of a scarf waving in the breeze, a back receding into the distance. Smoothly threading its way through the steady stream of Volkswagens, the figure crossed the wide avenue to the trolley stop on the other side. I tried to cross too, but with so many cars whizzing by I couldn't get across. By the time three big trucks had rumbled by, blocking my view, Mayakovsky had disappeared, but when I finally managed to cross over to the trolley stop, which was called Tschaikowskistrasse, I discovered a bar in front of it, with an open door. I peered in to see *her* sitting at a table right in the middle, looking at me. It couldn't be. I rubbed my eyes, took a closer look, and saw that it was Lilya. That well-built, dapper man next to her must be her husband, Osip B. His clean-shaven cheeks glowed with confidence, and his eyes were bright—sharp but not cold. Using long division as a metaphor, if that brightness was the dividend, with either determination or a sense of responsibility the divisors, what was left over would be the sort of longing I saw in his eyes. The burliness of his chest was proportionate to the size of his fortune, and his freshly shined shoes gleamed like the backs of Japanese rhinoceros beetles.

"Lilya," he called, and the woman grasped his arm, placing her cheek on his shoulder, sweetly whispering "Osip" in his ear. Yet all the while she was looking straight at me, sending me a come-hither look. She must have thought I was Mayakovsky. I couldn't forgive her for sidling up to Osip that way while continuing to flirt with me.

"You promised me you'd be where we'd agreed at four o'clock, and here you are," I said, loud enough for her husband to hear. Perhaps it was his old lover Maria rather than Lilya he'd agreed to meet at four, but that didn't matter anymore. My heart was full of Mayakovsky's pure anger, and as his spokesman, I was determined to torment this woman.

Ignoring what I'd said, and with a sticky sort of smile, Lilya peered into her husband's eyes. The smile Osip gave her in return was tender, all-embracing; then he turned to me with the same kind look in his eyes and asked, "Did you get some poems written?" He wasn't the least bit jealous. While he was definitely convinced that I was Mayakovsky, it apparently didn't occur to him that I might steal his wife. I now saw something of *her* in Osip.

"Have something to eat with us," Osip said to me-as-Mayakovsky. I sat down in the third chair—the empty one—at their table. Giving my bouquet of bright red roses to Lilya didn't feel right somehow, so I handed them to Osip.

"These are wonderful roses," he said, his face lighting up. "Roses only you could write. What's more, they don't seem like merely personal roses. They have the power to change our whole society. Consider this a small token of thanks," he said, casually taking a roll of bills out of his pocket and handing it to me. I took it without thinking. What country's money it was I couldn't say, but as I had never held a roll of bills like this, as thick as a dictionary, my heart was pounding. Mayakovsky as played by me was rather pathetic, happily taking money from his rival.

"You're awfully thin. Have you been getting enough to eat? I'll treat you, so have a good nourishing supper tonight." Osip was genuinely worried about Mayakovsky. Just as she is always concerned about my health. But now I was Osip's rival in love. This whole situation made me unbearably angry. Lilya couldn't have forgotten how cornered she'd felt, unable to endure the emptiness of bourgeois life until that day when, craving the poet's body, she'd pounced on him, clinging to him as if she were having some kind of fit. Yet now she was cuddling up to her husband as if none of that had ever happened.

The man did have qualities that Mayakovsky lacked: he had a stable income, he granted small favors easily, he was clean and well groomed, he liked children—that sort of thing. Nothing that a poet needed to envy him for. Feeling very nasty, I blurted out, "Your wife has a tendency to be attracted to bohemians—she wants to lose herself in dangerous love affairs. Don't you think she might run off with an artist one of these days?"

"Oh, my," he laughed, putting his arm around his wife's shoulder, "what a naughty girl." He sounded awfully affected but didn't seem to be putting on an act.

I noticed Osip's leather briefcase lying on a side table—the sort of case a businessman would carry. The clasp was open, so I could see the spines of the books inside. The names Tolstoy and Dostoyevsky, printed in gold, glittered in the light. Did Osip love both of these literary masters at the same time? I'd never before met anyone who did. Perhaps he'd just picked two volumes at random to add some weight to his briefcase. Or were these books a sort of talisman he carried around, for security? I was getting more and more frustrated. Mayakovsky might have been angry enough to knock the briefcase off onto the floor.

Lilya leaned back in her chair and crossed her legs. The hem of her skirt floated up to reveal her thigh, white as a fish's belly, all the way up to the lace trimming of her slip. Taking a rose from the bouquet, she started tickling her own thigh with it. Her eyes were trained on me. The rose petals lapped at the skin of her thigh like a dog's tongue. The flower gradually slid up until it slipped inside her skirt and began tickling between her legs. From his angle, her husband couldn't see what she was playing at. Mayakovsky was being tempted. I had to say something. If I opened my mouth, shocking insults might come pouring out. Perhaps that was exactly what Lilya was hoping for. Maybe she wanted to watch a fight between her husband and her lover. The sight of them fighting would be evidence of how deeply she was loved—she wanted to devour that. But I wouldn't let her get away with it. Ignoring her, I calmly turned to Osip and smiled.

"If it wasn't for you, I wouldn't be able to write my poems," I said. "I don't think there's anyone as important to me as you."

"My friendship with you is actually much deeper than any romantic love," he replied, his face as sweet as a donkey's. Osip was disgusted with himself for allowing his carnal love for a woman to control his life, and one of his true desires was for a firm foundation, based on friendship with a man. What he said was not a lie—it was just that he had any number of true desires.

Apparently unable to understand this, Lilya, her brow furrowed in a fit of pique, threw the rose onto the floor and started stomping it to pieces with the spike of one high-heeled shoe.

"What are you doing?" shouted Osip, picking up the rose. "Such a terrible waste of a beautiful flower!"

"There are so many," Lilya replied with a snort, "it doesn't matter if I throw one away. Now that you've paid for them, we can do whatever we please with them."

"You just live off someone else's money like a parasite—you don't even write poetry." It was a terrible thing to say, an insult to the woman before me. But wasn't that woman actually me? The only reason I'd been able to say such dreadful things was that I'd been addressing them to me. Lilya started bawling like a lousy actress. After a moment's hesitation, Osip apparently decided that he'd better take his wife's side and, turning to me, shouted, "Get out. Right now." While his lips were trembling, his eyes weren't the least bit angry. They seemed full of pity for the poor, hungry poet who would now be left to wander the streets.

Being driven out of the bar was no cause for despair. I like the outdoors. During the day, if I'm inside for more than two hours, I want to go out. I'm sure the words in poems feel that way sometimes, too—that instead of being shut up in a book or a library or in someone's study, they would rather be on a poster somewhere, exposing themselves to the city.

There were posters on the wall of the trolley stop.

"PHARMACISTS GIVE US MEDICINE—NOT POISON BUT A BALM FOR WOUNDS!"

What could this poster be advertising? It seemed a little off target for a pharmaceutical ad, yet too sophisticated for an antidrug campaign.

"OUT OF IMPOSSIBLE LOVE GROWS THE FEVER THAT DISSOLVES SOCIETY, GRADUALLY CHANGING IT."

Was this an ad for a movie? Or a campaign poster for the next election?

When you take stiff, propaganda-like slogans and pick them apart, you sometimes discover their origins in places you would never have expected.

Then I had an idea—I'd print a private message on

posters, which I'd put up all over the city. By putting a letter addressed to only one person on a poster, and exposing it to the public eye, inside and outside would be reversed, and the city, now as interior as a warm heart, might surround me, wrapping me in an embrace. This is what my poster would say: "2:00, 3:00, 4:00, I'VE BEEN WAITING ALL THIS TIME BUT YOU DIDN'T COME. THE CITY AND I ARE NOW ONE, BODY AND SOUL. I WILL NOT BE COMING HOME. GOODBYE, GOODBYE."

When I came to myself, I was standing on the verge of the forest. I turned around to see that the Majakow-skiring was still close by. I could easily go back there if I wanted to. The street separating the city from the forest rose before me like a sinister band of light. I'd been so attached to the city, I thought I'd never be able to leave it. But I'd easily stepped outside the *Ring*. For no particular reason, I had assumed that outside the city all would be desolation and loneliness, but I seem to have been mistaken. The smell of dry grass, steaming in the hot sun, and the buzzing of bees like tiny stitches, sewing everything up. The earth is sweet, and every time the breeze goes by its fingers play in my hair and gently stroke my cheeks. What season is caressing my skin? It feels good. Who would have known that parting could be this pleasant, as fine as spring?

PUSCHKINALLEE

When I got off the Ringbahn at Treptower Park Station, the heat and humidity suddenly disappeared—I was washed in fresh air. There was a kiosk outside the train station where men were drinking beer. People were streaming into a big store selling trees and shrubs to plant in gardens. Alone under the elevated tracks, I noticed something alarming: my body had shrunk to the size of a child's. Being so small I was afraid I'd be attacked from behind before I got through this passage under the tracks; besides, once I was outside I didn't know how I'd manage with no one to take me by the hand. But I was not a child anymore, and even when I'd been one there was no war on, I told myself, which calmed me down a bit. There were no houses, or post offices, or road signs here, only plane trees lining the avenue on both sides as far as I could see. They were so tall I only seemed smaller. I was not Alice in Wonderland.

The trunks of the plane trees were pale and looked so smooth I wanted to touch them, but something standoffish about them kept me from reaching my hand out. They were mottled, with lighter and darker gray patches that fitted together like a puzzle. I remembered seeing military uniforms with a similar pattern at a souvenir shop.

The leaves were completely outside my line of vision,

but when I tilted my chin straight up I saw them covering the sky overhead, so green I wanted to squeeze the juice out of them. They swayed in the breeze, close enough to the sun to absorb its light and deliver it straight down the trunks. The leaves were large and floppy, overlapping, though each one was thin enough to see through.

Obeying the law of perspective, the plane trees headed toward the vanishing point, growing smaller and smaller as they got farther and farther away. I'd grown so dependent on such scenes, with the size of things adjusted to fit me, that perhaps I'd been living under the delusion that I was the biggest thing around. But I wasn't big at all—it just looked that way because I was nearest. *Near*, of course, meant near from my point of view, which was only natural since I was the one looking, but this being the case, the only way to figure out where I actually was would be to start from the vanishing point and watch the trees get gradually taller and taller until they reached full size: that would be the only way—and not a very dependable one, either—to define my position.

I thought this sort of magnificent tree-lined avenue could only be found in an oil painting hanging in some art museum. Without an emperor in a horse-drawn carriage, the scene didn't look right somehow. The Mercedes Benz now driving between the trees looked as small as a toy. And because Germany no longer has an emperor, I wanted to ask these pale soldier-trees standing at attention who they were waiting for. In this emperorless age, only a dictator pretending to be some kind of famous celebrity would ride down this road in a convertible with the top down, waving to the people.

All the trees bent ever so slightly toward the center of the avenue, and a few were leaning so far over they seemed about to break in the middle. They reminded me of drunks standing by the side of the road, trying to keep from vomiting. If these plane trees threw up, greenish yellow gunk mixed with bits of undigested insect wings would glop down on the shiny black hood of the Mercedes Benz that just happened to be passing beneath them.

A father with hairy legs protruding from his shorts and his five- or six-year-old daughter, wearing a helmet and riding a miniature bicycle, hurried down the broad bicycle path between sidewalk and street. Every time her father looked back at her the girl threw her shoulders back and stuck out her chest. She was pedaling awfully fast for such a little girl. The pleats of her light blue cotton dress swam lightly around her thighs. Summer vacation. The moment the words came into my head, the sweltering heat of my memory pulled me back in time, reducing me to the size of an elementary school pupil. This was not Berlin, but the flower bed in that schoolyard in northern Tama on the outskirts of Tokyo. The sunflowers were a little taller than me, so I had to reach up to stick my fingernails between the closely gathered seeds to pull one out, and then I'd tuck it into the pocket of my shorts. Each time I put my hand in my pocket, the thread unraveling from the seam inside got tangled around the tips of my sweaty fingers. I planned to feed these sunflower seeds to my hamster when I got home, but sometimes I'd bite the edge of one with my back teeth to open it so I could chew on the slender, grayish bit inside. Once home, I heard the words "Anniversary of the War's End" coming from the television. Though I had always thought I lived in peacetime, when I was born the war had only been over for fifteen years. What if I had been alive during the war—just the thought made me shiver. It wasn't bombs I was afraid of, but the military police. "This government keeps fighting a war they know they can't win—the people who are dying don't mean any more to them than the logs burning in their fireplace," someone might overhear me say in a coffee shop, and that night Nazi MPs would come to arrest me ... but what's this? ... they have Japanese faces. Couldn't be. This is Berlin, isn't it? I'd thought this was a safety zone, but now I wasn't sure; seeking solace in yellow I found a dandelion, but then the purple thistles around it started to gleam, burning with hostility. Realizing that I'd come to a full stop, I started walking again. One step into the latticelike pattern of the plane trees cast shadows on the ground and I felt the cool air; with the next step, the dry sunlight was burning my cheeks.

There was a grassy lawn the size of a soccer field on either side of the tree-lined avenue. Way back and over to the right somewhere there was supposed to be a girl named Berlin, but she was hidden behind the trees so I couldn't see her from here. When I see big parks like this I feel free and open one minute and unsettled the next. Once a town starts forming, the land is covered with more and more houses, and though patches of open land might be left, surrounded by barbed wire, there usually aren't any grassy fields that don't belong to anyone. Could something be buried underneath? Sometimes parks are planted with flower beds in areas that were once borderlands. So maybe under this field is the blood of people who were shot trying to cross the border, I thought, but then decided I must be wrong. That couldn't be it. The line of death that had separated East and West Berlin was along the river some ways away from here, while this whole memorial park is on the Eastern side.

People were lying on the grass gazing up at the sky; others—practicing yoga?—with their foreheads resting on their hands, flat on the ground, had their bottoms sticking up in the air. A couple sitting back to back, each reading a book, formed a perfect X when I looked at them from the side. No big, noisy groups at all. This was a place where people came to be alone, or alone with one other person.

I'd wanted to come here with her, but knowing she'd refuse, I hadn't even bothered to ask. She wouldn't want to come this far into the East. A grassy field in a park is just the same whether it's in East or West Germany, but that's exactly what makes the name of the park a sticking point. Traveling through this part of Berlin to get to this field would also be a problem—there's way too much of that old Cold War atmosphere around here.

To the left of the tree-lined avenue I saw red and yellow flower beds and a fountain that took me back in time. This sort of park was often featured on old Soviet postcards. The pale blues, lurid yellows, and dark reds I remembered from printed materials back in the 1970s rose up, superimposing themselves on the scene before me. Of course, socialism didn't change the colors of grass and flowers, but on postcards they certainly looked different back then. Even now, with Germany unified, those colors from the past will sometimes reappear, just for a moment, on plants.

Suddenly a strong wind arose, blowing the dark clouds that had been lying along the horizon up into the sky to hide the sun. When I looked around, the people on the grass had disappeared, and no one was cycling or walking either. Opposite the fountain, across the avenue was the main gate to the memorial park. There probably wouldn't be any pavilions where I could take shelter in the park, but not wanting to just stand here getting soaked in a sudden shower, I hurried on, figuring that after meeting that girl, being rained on would be a little less miserable.

Inside the gate I saw soldiers in khaki uniforms walking toward me. Seemingly unaware that an evening shower was about to fall, they strode toward me in groups of two or three, laughing and talking. They were probably on their way back from the Soviet War Memorial. When I got close enough to make out what they were saying, I realized they must be American GIs.

My whole body stiffened. I didn't remember ever seeing this many American soldiers together at one time. If I had, it was probably in a movie or on TV, a story set in some other time, which I saw not as myself but through the eyes of a person from Okinawa, or Korea, or Vietnam, fearfully watching the American soldiers. No wonder I was so tense. If someone had suddenly asked me what year it was, I would have felt uneasy naming a year beyond 2000. And if asked where I was, the idea of being in a city far from Asia would have seemed as unreal as a fairy tale. The place where I now stood shook, then melted, its outlines unclear. Inside I tensed up, then broke down, felt feverish then cold and hard even as I kept walking at the same pace, trying to hide this turmoil, my eyes trained on a point far in the distance, expressionless.

More and more soldiers walked out of the park—apparently, quite a large group had come to see the memorial. The trees were perfectly silent, standing at attention in rows like soldiers while the real soldiers did as they pleased, zigzagging along, stopping now and then to wave their arms around, completely absorbed in the stories they were telling. There was something strange about that. They all looked so cheerful.

This park is a memorial to Red Army troops who died in the war. Historians give various estimates so no one knows exactly how many, but apparently more Russians died in the war against Nazi Germany than in any other. These lives were literally lost in Berlin. And there is no way to return them to their owners.

But mourning dead soldiers couldn't be the sole purpose of this huge memorial. If you want to show reverence for a dead person, sprinkling a handful of sand over the grave should be enough. That huge statue of a Russian soldier was built so that no one would forget it was the Soviet Union that saved Berlin from Nazi Germany, and that countless Russians had died defending this city. Even so, Berliners believe they were saved by America. Or maybe England, but definitely not Russia, because even back then Russia was their enemy.

I saw no cold sneers or faces flushed with anger; in fact, these Americans looked as happy as a group of junior high school kids who are done gawking at the Great Buddha at Nara and are now on their way to dinner. "Looks like you're on vacation," I wanted to say. "What do you think this monument means?" If I'd asked one of them, he might have politely shared his thoughts, but I was still much too nervous to speak.

When the long line of soldiers finally petered out, my tension eased and I felt much better, but now I was alone again. That would have been fine if I'd been walking on a beach. But all by myself in this artificially constructed square park, I felt as if I'd wandered into a hiding place for state secrets, which unsettled me. I'm not a spy or a journalist—what is this place anyway? I had no idea when I meandered in, but I'll leave right away, really, I'm just an ordinary person. This string of excuses rang hollow in my ears, keeping time with the sound of my footsteps. I stopped to shake them off. I was being ridiculous. There were no state secrets here. Just the opposite. This was a public memorial, built in the hope of everyone coming see it.

The center of the memorial was shaped like a huge rectangle; it faced a hill, some distance away, something like an ancient Japanese tomb mound. Even from this far away the soldier standing on top of it looked so big that he must have been about half the size of the Brandenburg Gate.

Right beside me was a stone statue of a mother. Her head was bowed, the fist on her chest tightly clenched. Looking up at this massive statue—she stood on a base at about eye level—I tried talking to her. "Did you lose your son?" I asked. "Was he shot on the battlefield?" The stone statue said nothing in reply. If her head had bowed a little lower, and then, no longer able to support herself, she had bent over double, perhaps I would have been pierced right through with pure sadness and hopelessness. But, though it might seem rude to say so, there was something defiant about this woman. In the angle of her neck I saw the pose of someone aware of people watching her, and her clenched fist showed not so much the unbearable sadness of a grieving mother as her pride in fulfilling her duty to endure. Her lower body gradually stopped being human and became part of the unmovable stone pedestal. The creases in her skirt looked as solemn and proud as the national flag. "You look awfully sad," I said. The statue of the mother glowered down at me but said nothing. On the verge of saying something really rude, like, "You wouldn't actually be feeling proud of yourself for having sacrificed your son to your country, would you?" I quickly swallowed the words, but apparently she heard me anyway. Tears glinted in the eyes of the statue. Or that's what I thought until I realized that big raindrops had fallen into the mother's eyes. Rather than turning into tears and rolling down her cheeks, the raindrops disappeared, absorbed by the stone. Stone apparently has that much absorptive power. Even though it looks so hard. As the rain soaked her cheeks, the lines around the mother's mouth stood out starkly and her eyebrows raised until finally, moving her shoulders back and forth as if she were rowing a boat, she lifted her head. She was now staring straight down on me. Stiffening with fear, I drew my head back, but for some reason found myself growing angrier and angrier. "You didn't actually *encourage* your son to go to war, did you?" I asked, itching for a fight, but my head ended up only hitting a wall of silence. Being made of stone, it wasn't particularly strange that she didn't reply, but still I couldn't forgive her. And there was something else irritating me. The rain was pouring down now, tangling my wet hair like a cold hand moving around my head. It was so persistent, I felt as if it were touching my skull. "The Egoist Party dragged your son off to the war, didn't they?" I was now a high school girl, screaming my protests at the world. "You voted for the Egoist Party, knowing they'd send the sons of everyone who didn't belong to the party to war, didn't you? Why did you do that?" The rain streamed down my cheeks, and no matter how many barbs I threw at her it was no use. Now that she'd turned completely to stone, this mother looked as if she'd never even heard that her son was dead, yet at times she had felt terribly sad and, sitting there, a grieving mother with her head bowed, tried to bear the pain, but then it always rained, and with people praising her all the time, saying her son had died for his country, she'd finally given up, deciding it was easier to be as hard as rock for all eternity.

Fewer and fewer raindrops came plopping down until finally they stopped altogether, leaving only the dark sky. The huge gravestones lined up on either side of the memorial park turned out not to be gravestones at all, but a picture book carved on sixteen slabs of stone. Relief carvings with text were lined up along both sides. The park was laid out so that as you read the book, looking at the pictures, page by page, you gradually got closer to the huge statue of the Russian soldier. The same story was told on eight slabs, in German on one side and in Russian on the other. Perhaps those American soldiers I'd seen a while back hadn't been able to read either text, which might explain why they were in such a good mood.

The story begins with Nazi Germany's first attacks, rolling eastward to steal territory from other countries. The carvings of military planes flying in the sky are crudely done, on purpose. Even elementary school kids draw cartoons that look much better. "I'd sure hate to be drawn this badly," said a voice from behind, and I turned around to see a tall, thin youth who looked like he'd come straight from trendy Shibuya. "Hey, take a look at this," he said, holding up his computer screen like a hand mirror to show me a photograph. A dung beetle crawling across the desert, I thought, but what he said next turned things completely upside down: "The whole world's amazed that Japan has these state-of-the-art tanks."

"A tank?" I asked. "So insects are called 'tanks' in Japan. There's something nice about a country where they sell bell crickets in department stores but don't have a single tank, don't you think?" I blurted out, then peered into the guy's face but saw no reaction; besides, what would a Japanese tourist be doing here in the first place? Was he really here, or ... I was blinking furiously, trying to think. What was even more surprising was that his face didn't really look all that young; in fact, the longer I stared at him, the older he got—thirty, thirty-five, forty, forty-five. "Those planes carved on the panel look like flies, don't they?" I said, but maybe he didn't hear me because in lieu of an answer he showed me the next picture on his screen, practically drooling as he said, "Here's the kind I really like."

I gasped at what I saw: a laughing girl in a military uniform, straddling a propeller plane that looked just like a fat, dark green caterpillar. Though her face was young—about junior high school age—her breasts, enlarged with silicone, bulged so beneath her middy blouse they seemed about to explode. Since it's illegal to send bombs through the mail, she must have been taking the girl next door somewhere in her plane—legally, of course. I gave the guy a slap on the arm and, pointing to the stone picture book said, "Why don't you take a look at this?"

A woman running, holding her child; a man with his fist raised in fury as he ran; another woman, also running, her face covered with both hands. The picture might have come from an illustrated Bible, but with military planes in the sky it couldn't be a scene from ancient times. A woman sitting on the ground, both hands thrust into the air as she looked up at the sky. Another fallen, lying on her back. The stone picture book was now telling about the Nazi invasion.

Unlike the crudely sketched warplanes, the faces of these people on the run looked positively noble, the skilled carving showing the sculptor's confidence. As if he were saying, "I studied Greek sculpture and Rodin, too." Still, I didn't feel like talking to these people. Their faces were much too well balanced. They didn't look like the kind of people I'd want to make friends with. I simply can't trust someone whose face isn't a bit off-kilter because she's shy or maybe too softhearted. These people were born in the country of stone, and they'd stay in stone forever. If their hearts were touched by a living human being, the stone would melt and the memorial's message would lose its clarity. I started to feel sorry for them, all staring straight ahead that way, not allowed even a wrinkle or two around their noses. And since they all had the same build, there were no physical characteristics to mark them as individuals. Dressed like laborers, their muscles were so perfectly balanced that I couldn't imagine what sort of specific work each one did.

Having wandered into the world of relief, half trapped in stone and half sticking out of it, I wanted to read a newspaper to find out what was going on, but here that would be impossible. There are no daily newspapers in the country of stone. Which meant there was no way to find out things like how many had died yesterday, or what sort of conference would be held tomorrow. So what should I do? Suddenly it occurred to me that I should try to help the injured, so I looked around for someone lying on the ground, needing first aid. But for a scene of carnage, everything was awfully orderly.

The stone people stopped their lamentations and, with furrowed brows, began to think about the meaning of war. Until now, the words they'd used most in their daily lives were the names of their children, or of flowers and other plants, or of the dogs they kept, or of carpentry tools or parts of the machines they used, but now, the name of their homeland was suddenly more important than any of these things. That was what they had to think of, and once it was firmly planted in their minds, they repeated it over and over again. They had nothing else to depend on. The bombs kept falling, destroying their houses. Their cows died, their workshops were flattened, their fields burned. Under this barrage, why couldn't they find some raw, living words to toss back and forth? When a simple doubt, like, "Why must we kill each other when we all belong to the same human race?" could easily have been rolled into a ball to throw to their neighbors.

I heard fragments of a speech from somewhere far off. "My brothers, the army of Nazi Germany is attacking. They have invaded Ukraine, Belarus, Latvia, Lithuania, Estonia, and Moldova, and have begun to enslave the workers there." Perhaps the speaker was using an old-fashioned megaphone, for the voice crackled and was hard to make out. Even with bombers flying overhead, this speaker was taking his time, carefully pronouncing the name of each ethnic nation-state, already thinking beyond this battle to postwar Europe. After the war, when forests, towns, and wounded citizens are all spoils for the taking, a new age, truly delicious for the victors, begins. So that there would be no doubt about which cakes he had every right to claim as his own, he was now naming each cake his army had saved from the Nazis. "The Russian Red Army had to fight to save the Ukraine Tarte, the Belarus Crème, the Choco Latvia, the Estonia Clair, the Strawberry Shortcake, and many others from the dastardly Nazis." "Really?" said another voice. "Well then, I guess we'll just have to give them up." "We'll let you have the cakes you just listed, but the Nagasaki Castella, the Hiroshima Manjū, and Tokyo Thunder Crackers are ours." I turned around to see that one of those American soldiers from before was back. His smile gone, his ample chin now trembled with anger. But when he saw Stalin's stone head burst out of the bas relief like a ball of fire, he quickly ran away.

Hearing Stalin's voice listing cakes, the stone people hurriedly changed into ethnic costumes. Bright red flowers with emerald green leaves embroidered on billowing white collarless blouses over scarlet skirts trimmed with white lace, as sturdy white legs slid into crimson boots. I heard ethnic music, perhaps from the Ukraine. But where was it coming from? The dandelions at my feet had turned into speakers. The women, now all decked out in their costumes, put their hands on their hips and, swaying gently from side to side, began lightly tapping the ground with their heels. The sound brought men, also dressed in red and white ethnic costumes, up out of the earth to place their hands on the women's hips and start dancing along, moving their heads from side to side and then waving their arms in the air. Masks with pictures of laughing eyes and smiling mouths were pasted onto the faces of both men and women. The colors each ethnic group wore were much too bright; wondering why they all had to be so gaudy, I figured that this was to show that there were various groups, each one different from the others. These people were not just a motley assortment but a republic formed when all these groups came together. "But surely you didn't all have ethnic costumes stashed away? Where did you get them? Ah, you bought them at a souvenir shop? I understand—in fact, I bought the yukata I have with me at a souvenir shop in Narita Airport." As soon as I'd said that, the people stopped dancing, took off their costumes, and hurriedly changed back into their work clothes. "So you have to be ethnic sometimes," I said, "but you have to be laborers, too." They all went back to work. The shoemaker returned to his workshop and the baker to his oven, while the blacksmith picked up a huge hammer. But with a war going on, they couldn't very well settle down to business as usual. The baker shut up his shop, piled all the bread he'd just baked onto a cart, and took off for the battlefield. The soldiers were waiting for bread. The stone book had a picture of soldiers receiving sheaves of wheat, but raw wheat wouldn't do them much good—while they were threshing it, grinding the grain into flour, and kneading the dough, the enemy would attack. Soldiers' muddy boots were piled high on the table in the shoemaker's workshop, and he was cleaning the mud off them and pounding nails into the soles. His regular customers had brought smart leather shoes and high heels for him to repair, but he pushed all those out the window.

At the blacksmith's there was a basket overflowing with Suma-phones and Ai-phones: he was tossing them, one after another, into the fire. They had all been confiscated from ordinary citizens. These devices, so that they wouldn't feed the people misinformation, were now prohibited. But the blacksmith didn't leave them to burn; after a while he took them out again, putting them one by one on his anvil and pounding them flat. Then a dragonfly in welding glasses placed the flattened phones on a tray and flew them to a factory far to the back, where they were seen being made into metal helmets. These were not ordinary helmets, though: once they were put on, they attached themselves firmly to the human skull and could never be removed.

Now people were taking off their shoes. When they were barefoot, they slipped their jackets off, along with their trousers, and stuffed them all into large hempen sacks. "What are you doing?" I asked.

"We're giving our clothes to the soldiers," they said. "We want to give them everything. We've given them our clothes, our shoes, and all we own."

"But how will you live without your clothes?"

"We'll be fine, for our hearts have truly been washed clean."

"Were your brains washed as well?"

"Our brains, too, are clean. We are now blank slates once again."

I looked up at the sky and saw several huge metal flies circling overhead. Soldiers lined up and aimed their guns. They were so perfectly aligned they looked like the teeth on a zipper. They simply couldn't be human. I came back to myself with a start to find myself staring at a fly perched on the zipper of my handbag. When I slid the zipper open, the fly disappeared, leaving only the darkness inside.

"Really?" I heard a voice say in Japanese. That trendy young guy, straight from Shibuya, was standing beside me. "You gotta be kidding," he said. His eyes were narrowed in a forced smile with fear quickly spreading through it. Apparently, a soldier had told him that since he was so crazy about their military planes, he'd take him for a ride in one. "No thanks, I'm just fine, right here on the ground." I couldn't tell if this was his normal way of talking, or if he was trying to be funny. "Really—please don't go to all that trouble. I don't need to fly. Just my pics're plenty good enough for me." The soldier's eyes were hidden under his helmet; all I could see was the nervous trendy kid, trying to fend off this sudden invitation: "Like I said, I'm fine. Take someone else for a ride."

But the soldier wasn't going to give up that easily. "Didn't you hear me? I said I don't want to go up." Now he was getting irritated. He was mild-mannered at first, but he knows just when to get angry, I thought, strangely impressed, while at the same time frightened at the change in his voice. "Lay off," he said, "and quit trying to cram this military stuff down my throat. What's that? Duty, you say? You guys may be soldiers, but you're paid by a private corporation, aren't you? So what gives you the right to talk about duty? What? You belong to a government organization? You can't be serious. You're joking, right?" A storm seemed to be brewing. Spouting Shibuya slang, he told them he was just an anime-crazed kid, useless in wartime. Trying desperately to get away, wiggling his hips, he edged slowly backward as he rattled off excuses. "I mean, like, gimme a break—I don't even have a driver's license. A *pilot's* license? You gotta be crazy—nobody I know has a pilot's license. What? *Training?* Honest, I'm not cut out for that kinda stuff." His last step backward sent him tumbling silently into a huge hole that had opened up behind him.

Just as he disappeared, a pair of Russian soldiers walked slowly through the main gate carrying a huge wreath between them, holding it in both hands. Their faces were as white and translucent as wax, their lips a fiery red, their eyes blue as sapphires. Their uniforms looked freshly ironed. If they'd come all the way from Russia to pay their respects, it was a miracle their uniforms hadn't gotten wrinkled on the way. Or had they worn Adidas sportswear on the plane and changed at the hotel? Wondering if the bones of the dead, buried deep in the earth, would start rattling when they saw the wreath, I stared at the ground, but felt no stirrings.

Without exchanging a word, their faces perfectly solemn, the soldiers left. They could have played around a bit—after all, there were just the two of them, with no commanding officer around, and only me watching—but they must have thought there was a security mirror somewhere high in the sky, and they had to keep up their act until they were out of its range. I couldn't believe they were contemporaries of those American soldiers who'd been gabbing and laughing as they left the grounds.

The stone picture book was nearing its end now, with scenes of soldiers coming home from the war, welcomed by their families. A soldier face-to-face with his wife, who hands him a bouquet; though the flowers are laughing, the wife, seeing the darkness in her husband's expression, doesn't know what to do. The little boy with his arms around his father's waist cannot see his face. "Isn't it wonderful—your papa's home," the wife says to her children as if trying to quiet her own anxiety. He's completely changed: though she can't explain what's different about him, this is what she thinks to herself. The soldier himself is troubled. He was looking forward to coming home, but now that he's here, his family seem to be strangers. Though he takes off his uniform and scrubs his entire body, the feelings he had before the war do not come back. He has no words to describe the things he saw on the battlefield. And because he cannot talk about it, he's alone in his own house. He doesn't feel like going back to work, either. He wants to meet the guys he fought with in a bar somewhere and drink until morning. As if stripped of normal, everyday life, he is exhausted during the day and wakes up at night, night after night.

An ordinary photograph of this moment of homecoming could be ripped up and thrown away. On a digital camera, memories can be erased with a push of a button. But once they are honestly carved into stone, memories remain forever.

I climbed up the side of the hill, a mound of earth like an ancient tomb. I was probably meant to use the stone steps at the front, but I was afraid that that would make a believer of me before I'd found out what religion I was joining—all those statues and sarcophagi on the top of the hill made me suspicious, even if people said they had nothing to do with religion. Had I been told, "This is a Christian church," or "This is a Hindu temple," I'd have felt much more at ease.

I climbed slowly up the grassy slope. I had no one to mourn or commemorate. I had come to meet someone who wasn't dead yet, a little girl; she probably wasn't a little girl anymore, but surely she was still alive.

On top of the mound was a small shrine with a round dome like the *kamakura* snow huts children make in Japan; I peeked inside to see a group of people who might have come straight out of a religious painting. Two tough-looking men in military uniforms were draping a cloth with the word *slava* on it over something. The cloth shone brightly, as did the Cyrillic letters. *Slava* was Russian for "word" wasn't it? But the spelling was wrong. The first vowel should be an *o* instead of an *a*. Since the letters were so shiny, perhaps they said "luminous moss." Or "glory," maybe, or "power." But what kind? Was it the name of a battleship? Was it somehow related to the girl I was going to meet? These people couldn't have draped the cloth over her, treating her as if she were dead, could they? "Excuse me," I called out to them, but they didn't seem to hear. And as the lattice door was locked, I couldn't get inside.

I gave up. I stopped staring through the lattice door like one possessed and took a few steps backward to look up at the huge soldier. He was holding a little girl, hugging her close. She must have been left alone in the ruins. I felt his strength and purity as he protected this child. But what if she had been older, say, seventeen or so? Her body was small enough so that her bottom rested firmly in the soldier's hand, but her face, surrounded by curls as heavy as Bach's wig, looked older. Her bottom was simply too small. Or perhaps her head was too big for the rest of her. "Hey," I called out to her, "it looks like your head grew up but your body stayed small—is that it?" Startled, she looked down at me. It would take courage to jump down from that height. And if she did jump there were still pieces of a broken swastika scattered on the ground which might hurt her feet. But if she stayed where she was, the soldier would have to be a soldier forever, and she would be stuck in the body of a child with the face of a grown woman. They couldn't go on this way.

The girl braced herself and jumped. I drew my head back and closed my eyes. I was holding my breath, waiting for a crash, but when I heard a refreshingly clean thud right next to me I opened my eyes to see that, having made a splendid landing, she was already running across the lawn. I hurried after her. The girl's bouncing curls changed from gray stone to brown hair, growing lighter and lighter until she was a blonde whose chubby arms and legs were firming up and putting on muscle by the time we left the park and were running down the tree-lined avenue, past cars, past that Mercedes-Benz, her legs developing voluptuous curves as we raced by the station where the men drinking beer at the kiosk looked up to ogle her, but by the time we crossed the street, ignoring the red light, her blonde hair was white, yet even so she kept on running, heading for the present, finally reaching the end of Pushkin Allee, easily crossing that bridge you couldn't have crossed without getting shot during the Cold War, and even with blue veins starting to stand out on her calves and with the skin on her heels about worn through, she didn't slow down, no, with the sweat pouring down her now-wrinkled forehead she laughed, and gasped, now a seventy-five-year-old woman racing into Kreuzberg.